Disney's

PIRATES of the CARIBBEAN
THE CURSE OF THE BLACK PEARL

Book of the Film

This is a Parragon book
First published in 2006

Parragon
Queen Street House
4 Queen Street
Bath, BA1 1HE, UK

ISBN 1-40548-319-9
Printed in Italy

Disney's
Pirates of the Caribbean
THE CURSE OF THE BLACK PEARL

Book of the Film

Adapted by Irene Trimble
Still photography by
Elliott Marks and John Bramley

Based on the screenplay
by Ted Elliott and Terry Rossio
and Jay Wolpert
Produced by Jerry Bruckheimer
Directed by Gore Verbinski

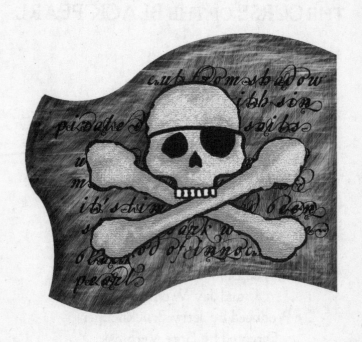

Chapter
1

Listen here: long ago, there was a legend of a ghostly black ship that sometimes appeared when the fog grew thick. Aye, its sails were big and black – as though they had been cut from shadow and sewn with sin. The timbers had been stained dark with the blood of innocent souls unlucky enough to cross the black ship's path. And its crew, it was said, were pirates all, cursed to sail forever under a foul wind of murder and mischief.

But of course, a tale like that would be nothin' but a sailor's old ghost story. And you don't believe in ghosts . . . do you?

The fog was dreadful. Still, the pride of the Royal Navy, the HMS *Dauntless*, kept its course.

Armed with 50 guns and a crew tough enough to make any pirate take pause, the *Dauntless* swept slowly onwards through the dark sea.

Standing alone at the ship's bow was its youngest passenger. Elizabeth Swann was her name. Her small hands clutched the rail as she shivered in the cold. Elizabeth was not a bit afraid of what might lie in wait in the fog. She secretly thought it would be exciting to meet a real pirate. She remembered a song from long ago, and slowly, into the grey mist, she began to sing:

"*Yo ho, yo ho, a pirate's life for me,*
Yo ho, yo ho, a pirate's life–"

Suddenly, a hand reached out and clutched her shoulder. "Quiet, missy!" snarled a seaman. "Cursed pirates sail these waters! You want to call 'em down on us?"

Elizabeth, then only 12 years old, stared wide eyed into the weather-beaten face.

"Mr Gibbs!" Captain Norrington snapped at the old sailor.

"But she was singin' about pirates," Gibbs

protested. "Bad luck to sing about pirates with us mired in this unnatural fog . . . mark my words."

Elizabeth knew that she was expected to behave. She was on her way to Port Royal, Jamaica, where her father was going to be governor. "We must comport ourselves as befits our class," he reminded her as he joined her on deck. Elizabeth nodded, but in her heart, she still wished to meet a pirate one day.

Quietly, she looked back out over the rail and stared into the deep green water. Suddenly, she noticed something afloat on the waves. It was a parasol – a sight that much delighted Elizabeth. She was wondering where it could have come from when a much larger shape slowly floated out on the foam. "Look!" she shouted, pointing over the side. A still body was now drifting towards the ship.

Captain Norrington reacted quickly. "Man overboard!" he shouted.

But Elizabeth could see that it wasn't a man. "Boy overboard!" she added, recognizing the person in the water to be someone about her own age.

"Fetch a boat hook and haul him out of there!" Captain Norrington ordered the men on deck. Elizabeth watched the crew of the *Dauntless* swing the boat hooks and snag the limp body as it passed the ship.

Governor Swann helped Captain Norrington drag the boy aboard as Elizabeth moved in for a closer look.

"He's still breathing!" declared Norrington, his ear down by the boy's mouth.

"But where did he come from?" asked Governor Swann.

The men of the *Dauntless* stood silent. The eyes of every crewman were searching the sea for an answer when Gibbs suddenly gasped. "Mary, mother of God!"

Looking out on the water, Elizabeth could now see the wreckage of a ship, along with the bodies of its crew. Then, slowly emerging from the fog, came the charred and burning hull of the doomed ship itself.

Captain Norrington, fearing it was all the work of pirates, quickly ordered his men to prepare for battle. "Move the boy aft!" he shouted.

"We need to clear the deck!"

Governor Swann pried Elizabeth's hand from the ship's rail and moved her away from the terrible sight. "He's in your charge," he said grimly to her as two sailors moved the boy's body behind the ship's wheel. "You'll watch over him."

Elizabeth nodded to her father. She went and knelt beside the boy as her father hurried away. She brushed his hair gently away from his forehead. The boy's eyes fluttered open.

"My name is Elizabeth Swann," she told him, taking his hand in hers.

"Will Turner," whispered the boy.

"I'm watching over you," she said, trying to comfort him, but the boy slipped back into unconsciousness.

The boy's movements had opened the collar of his shirt, and Elizabeth saw that he was wearing a gold chain with a medallion. She tugged it free from his neck and turned it over in her hand, hoping it might provide her with a clue to his identity. To her amazement, there, etched into the metal, was a skull and crossbones!

"Why, you're a pirate!" she whispered.

Elizabeth quickly hid the medallion under her coat as Captain Norrington passed by.

"Did he speak?" he asked, standing over Will's body.

"His name is Will Turner," she replied. "That's all I found out."

"Very good," said Captain Norrington, and moved on.

When Elizabeth felt sure the captain would not return, she took the gold medallion from her coat to give it one more look. But a sight that left her too frightened to move or cry out suddenly claimed all her attention. Through the fog came a tall ship with great black sails. From its topmost mast it flew a flag – a skull and crossbones! And as the ship slipped back into the fog to escape the cannon fire of the *Dauntless*, the skull on the pirate flag seemed to turn toward Elizabeth and smile.

Chapter
2

At the sound of a loud knock, Elizabeth's eyes suddenly snapped open. She was in her own bed, safe in the governor's mansion. She wondered for a moment if she had been dreaming. Then she turned up the flame of the oil lamp beside her bed and opened the small drawer of her jewellery box. There it was: the gold medallion she had secretly taken from Will Turner's neck eight years ago.

"Still in bed at this hour?" called Governor Swann as he continued to knock on the door.

Elizabeth quickly put on the necklace, threw on her dressing gown and opened the door for her father.

"It's a beautiful day," he announced as he walked in carrying a large box, "and I have a gift for you!"

Elizabeth's maid entered the room behind him and pulled back the heavy curtains, letting in the blue sky and morning light of Port Royal. It was a small, neat town on a snug harbour, guarded by the cannons of Fort Charles, which stood at the edge of the sea.

Governor Swann opened the box and held up an elegant velvet gown. "I thought you could wear it to the ceremony today," he said as Elizabeth, delighted with the gift, took the gown behind a dressing screen. "Captain Norrington's promotion ceremony," he added.

"I knew it," answered Elizabeth, peeking out from behind the screen as her maid tightened her corset strings.

Elizabeth knew that her father favoured a marriage between her and Captain Norrington, but she was in no way interested.

"He is a fine gentleman," her father added, trying to sway her, "and he fancies you, you know."

Elizabeth stepped out from behind the screen and frowned. The dress was beautiful but much too tight. "I'm told it's the latest fashion in London," he said, smiling at his lovely daughter.

"Women in London must have learned not to breathe," commented Elizabeth as she tried to adjust the dress and take a breath.

A while later, Elizabeth was preparing to leave with her father when the butler announced a caller at the door.

Governor Swann descended the stairs to find a young man carrying a long presentation box waiting in the mansion's foyer. It was Will Turner, now a grown man of 20 and a blacksmith by trade.

"Ah, Mr Turner!" said Governor Swann. "It's good to see you again."

"Good day, sir," replied Will. "I have your order."

The governor was very anxious to see the sword that Will had brought him. He opened the box and smiled with satisfaction. The dress sword of gold and steel was going to be presented to Captain Norrington at the ceremony, and Will had done a fine job.

Will began to point out the craftsmanship and balance of the sword to the governor, but as he was doing so, he looked up and saw Elizabeth, who was coming down the stairs. She looked lovelier than ever. A wide smile spread across his face.

"Ah, Elizabeth! You look stunning!" said Governor Swann.

"It's so good to see you," Elizabeth said, greeting Will, her own smile betraying her feelings for the young swordsmith. "I dreamed about you last night. About the day we met. Do you remember?"

"I could never forget, Miss Swann," Will replied.

The direction the conversation was taking obviously did not please Governor Swann. He took the sword from Will and quickly escorted Elizabeth out of the door.

"Good day, Mr Turner," Elizabeth said, smiling once more at her handsome young friend.

She gathered her skirts and stepped into the

waiting carriage with her father. Will stood there watching the carriage until it disappeared into the busy streets of Port Royal.

Chapter
3

On the journey to Fort Charles, Elizabeth could see the HMS *Dauntless* at anchor in the sparkling harbour. It was there to protect the citizens of Port Royal from the threat of thieves and pirates. And in case the presence of the *Dauntless* was not enough to discourage any would-be lawbreakers, the skeletons of four pirates swung from the gallows overlooking the harbour. A fifth noose hung empty, its rope bearing a sign: PIRATES – YE BE WARNED!

The midday sun was blazing hot when Elizabeth and her father arrived at the fort. She truly regretted wearing such a heavy dress in the day's heat. But despite the weather, everyone in town had turned out in their best to see Captain Norrington promoted to the rank of commodore. Elizabeth and her father were escorted to their seats and the ceremony began.

All seemed well . . . but far below the cliff in a small, leaky bit of a boat stood one of the slyest pirates ever to sail the Spanish Main. Captain Jack Sparrow was his name. He gazed solemnly at the pirates' bones that hung from the gallows, and nodded his respects as he sailed by. Then, as he made his way farther into the port, he set his sights on the ships at anchor. Captain Jack had come to Port Royal with a mind to acquire a somewhat larger boat.

He took a long look at the *Dauntless*. And though he knew it was a powerful ship with its 50 guns, Jack's attention was drawn to something very different: the HMS *Interceptor*, a small, sleek vessel with rail guns, and a mortar in the middle of the main deck. It was tied up at the navy landing, below the cliffs of Fort Charles.

Jack never wasted time when he saw something he wanted. Smoothly, he sailed up to the dock.

The harbourmaster looked Jack over. "Hold up there, ye!" he shouted, not liking what he saw of the man or his leaking boat. "The mooring fee's a shilling, and I'll need to know your name."

Jack smiled as the harbourmaster's assistant opened his ledger for Jack to sign. "What do you say to *three* shillings, and we forget the name?" answered Jack, throwing the shillings onto the ledger.

The harbourmaster's expression changed, as though he had completely misjudged Jack. He reached over his assistant's shoulder and closed the ledger with a long, crooked finger. Then he stepped aside and said, "Welcome to Port Royal, *Mr Smith!*"

Giving the harbourmaster a half salute, Jack strapped on his sword and headed up the dock toward the *Interceptor*, smiling. It was turning out to be a fine day, he thought.

He found two sailors guarding the *Interceptor* when he strolled towards its gangplank. "This dock is off limits to civilians," one of the guards warned him.

"Sorry, I didn't know," said Jack as his ear

caught the music of the ceremony taking place at Fort Charles. He shielded his eyes from the bright sun and looked up. "Some sort of to-do at the fort, eh? You two weren't invited?"

"Someone has to make sure this dock is off limits to civilians," the guard answered as he looked at Jack in his tattered pirate's rags.

"Yes," agreed Jack. "That's a fine goal, I'm sure. This must be an important boat."

"Ship," snapped the guard. "Commodore Norrington'll use the Interceptor to hunt down the last dregs of piracy on the Spanish Lake. There's no ship that can match the Interceptor for speed."

"That so?" replied Jack casually. "I've heard of one. Supposed to be fast, nigh uncatchable. The Black Pearl?"

Both guards went silent at the mention of the legendary ship.

"There's no real ship as can match the Interceptor," argued the first guard.

"I've seen it," answered the other. "The Black Pearl is a real ship."

The two began to argue over the existence of the notorious Black Pearl, and they realized too late that Jack had disappeared from the dock.

"You!" the guard shouted to Jack, who was now standing at the wheel of the *Interceptor*. "Get away from there!"

"I'm sorry," Jack said innocently as the guards charged up the gangplank. "It's just that it's such a pretty boat . . . I mean ship."

"You don't have permission to be aboard! What's your name?" the guard demanded.

"Smith," answered Jack brightly.

"What's your business in Port Royal, Mr Smith? And no lies!"

"None? Very well," sighed Jack. "I confess: I intend to commandeer one of these ships, pick up a crew in Tortuga, go out and do a little honest pirating."

The guards looked confused. "I said no lies!"

"I think he's telling the truth," said the other guard. Meanwhile, Jack noticed a commotion up at the fort. A beautiful girl in a velvet gown was falling from the cliff into the water below!

Chapter
4

Commodore Norrington and Governor Swann leaned over the parapet and considered jumping off the cliff to save Elizabeth, but the dive would have meant certain death. "The rocks, sir! It's a miracle she missed them!" said a soldier, holding Norrington back.

Elizabeth had just been chatting with the commodore. He had told her that now that he had received his promotion, he wished to find a fine woman to be his wife. "You have become a fine woman," he had said, hinting strongly that he wished to marry her.

Elizabeth had gasped and told him she couldn't breathe, but not because of Commodore

Norrington's suggestion that she become his wife. The heat of the midday sun and the tightness of her dress had overcome her, and she had fallen over the wall of the fort in a faint, tumbling towards the water.

Commodore Norrington and Governor Swann rushed down the cliff to the harbour.

Captain Jack Sparrow eyed the whole event impatiently. "Aren't you going to save her?" he asked the two guards as Elizabeth splashed into the water.

Both men looked at Jack blankly. "I can't swim," confessed one. Apparently, neither could the other, who just shook his head.

"Sailors," huffed Jack, resenting the delay in stealing the *Interceptor*. "Fine," he said. He handed his belt and pistol to them. "Don't lose those."

Jack dived into the water and swam towards Elizabeth, who was gasping for air as she disappeared below the surface. She was sinking slowly in the dark water, her velvet gown surrounding her like a cloud, when Jack's arm suddenly grabbed her around the waist.

Jack was a mighty swimmer, but he couldn't bring Elizabeth to the surface. He quickly realized that the weight of Elizabeth's dress was pulling them down. He ripped at the buttons until the heavy, water-soaked dress fell away, and the two of them floated to the surface.

The guards helped Jack haul Elizabeth onto the dock. "She's not breathing," said one of the guards as he put his cheek to her nose and mouth.

"Move," commanded Jack, who suddenly took a knife from the guard's sheath and leaned over Elizabeth.

Then, to the shock of both guards, Jack took the blade and slit Elizabeth's corset down the middle. Elizabeth immediately began coughing and sputtering.

"I never would have thought of that," said the guard.

"Clearly you've never been to Singapore," said Jack with a devilish smile. He was about to ask Elizabeth how she was feeling when he suddenly felt a blade at his neck.

"On your feet!" said Commodore Norrington to Jack. The pirate thought of trying to explain his position, but he knew it looked bad.

"Elizabeth! Are you all right?" asked Governor Swann.

"Yes, yes, I'm fine," Elizabeth said to her father.

As Captain Norrington tightened his grip on Jack, he noticed a brand on the stranger's inner wrist: the letter *P*, and above it, a tattoo of a small bird in flight across water. "Well, well . . . a pirate," remarked Norrington. "Jack Sparrow, isn't it?" Norrington's guards drew their pistols.

"*Captain* Jack Sparrow, if you please," answered Jack.

"I don't see your ship . . . *Captain*," Commodore Norrington sneered.

"He said he'd come to commandeer one," said one of the guards, handing over Jack's belt and pistol. Norrington examined the pirate's possessions and snorted. He was unimpressed with Jack's pistol, which held only a single shot, and his compass, which didn't point north.

"You are without a doubt the worst pirate I have ever heard of," Norrington taunted.

"Ah, but you have heard of me," Jack said, smiling.

Norrington had seen enough of the man by now to know that he would hang him in the morning, along with whatever other pirates were in prison at Fort Charles. "Fetch some irons," he said in a flat tone.

"I must protest," Elizabeth said. "Pirate or not, this man saved my life!" But Commodore Norrington wasn't about to let Jack get away. The guards fastened manacles around Jack's wrists.

"Finally . . ." sighed Jack, and lightning-quick snapped the corset he still held. Its laces caught around the pistol in the guard's hand and sent it sailing into the water. The men were momentarily shocked as Jack wrapped the chain between his manacles tightly around Elizabeth's neck. The pistol of every sailor on the dock now pointed at Jack, but Commodore Norrington raised his hand to hold his troops back. Jack was using Elizabeth as a shield. Commodore Norrington feared she might be killed.

Jack ordered Elizabeth to grab his belt and pistol and began backing them down the dock. "You are despicable!" Elizabeth said as she struggled.

But Jack only smiled. "I saved your life; now you've saved mine," he said. "We're square."

Then Jack announced, "Gentlemen. M'lady. You will always remember this as the day you *almost* caught Jack Sparrow." And with that, he shoved Elizabeth away, grabbed a ship's rope, and swung high and wide. Captain Norrington carefully aimed his pistol at Jack and fired. His bullet hit the rope, and Jack fell from high in the rigging.

Jack tumbled, then snapped the manacle chain over a line and slid down it to the deck of the ship. In an instant, Jack jumped from the deck . . . and dashed away.

"On his heels!" shouted Norrington. A squad of sailors took off into the streets and alleys of Port Royal. The hunt for Jack Sparrow was on!

Now standing alone on the dock with his daughter, Governor Swann placed his coat around Elizabeth's shoulders. The air had suddenly grown cold, and a thick fog from the harbour began to gather at their feet.

Chapter
5

The search party moved cautiously down a narrow alleyway. The fog had rolled in, making it difficult to see. They looked everywhere, but there was no sign of the pirate.

Jack slipped out from his hiding place behind a large statue once he was sure the search party had passed. As he crept along, he tested the doors of a darkened blacksmith's shop. He smiled as the double doors slid easily open.

The forge was dark, lit by only a few lanterns. Jack could see that the walls were covered with chains and tools. He was about to thank his luck for the chance to use them to cut the manacles from his wrists when he was startled by a loud snort. In the corner, drunk and asleep, was Mr Brown, the blacksmith. Jack tiptoed over and poked him hard. But Mr Brown didn't move, he just snorted loudly again.

Satisfied that the man would cause him no trouble, Jack walked over to the furnace and lowered the chain between his wrists into the hot coals. When the chain began to glow red, Jack took a short-handled sledgehammer from the wall and with one hard stroke broke the manacle from one wrist. His arm was red and blistered, but his hands were finally free.

Jack was about to break the manacle from his other wrist when he heard the iron latch on the door move. Quickly, he dived for cover just as Will Turner stepped into the blacksmith's shop.

Will looked around the forge and saw old Mr Brown asleep in the corner. "Right where I left you," muttered Will. Then he looked at the sledgehammer lying on the furnace and said, "Hmm, not where I left you." Will was reaching to pick up the sledgehammer and put it in its proper place when a blade suddenly came out of the darkness and slapped his hand!

Will jumped back and came face to face with Jack Sparrow, who now had his sword levelled at Will's chest. Will looked him over from head to toe. "Why, you're the one they're hunting," he said, glaring at Jack. "The pirate!"

Will grabbed a sword lying next to the furnace and pointed it at Jack.

"Do you think this is wise, boy? Crossing swords with a pirate?" asked Jack. He was unhappy to see Will answer the question by raising his sword in attack.

Will and Jack thrust and cut at each other with lightning speed. "You know what you're doing, I'll give you that," said Jack as the two circled each other, Will keeping up with every move Jack made.

Jack moved until the door of the forge was at his back. Then, to Will's surprise, the pirate turned and made a run for it. Will reacted in an instant and threw his sword at Jack's back.

The sword flew over Jack's head and buried itself deep in the planks of the door. Jack pulled on the latch, but it was no good. The sword was in the way.

Will thought he had his opponent trapped. But Jack Sparrow always had another plan in his pocket. Slowly, he turned to Will and smiled.

Jack was now eyeing the back door of the blacksmith's shop. "That's a good trick. Except, once again, you are between me and the way out," he said, pointing his sword at the back door. "And now," he added confidently, "you have no weapon!"

Will simply took another sword from the rack and began to attack.

As Jack parried, he looked around and noticed that the shop was filled with weapons. "Who makes all these?" he asked.

"I do," Will answered as their swords clashed and rang again. "And I practise with them three hours a day!"

"You need to find yourself a girl . . . or maybe the reason you practise three hours a day is you've found one but can't get her?" Jack teased.

"I practise three hours a day so when I meet a pirate, I can kill him!" Will answered angrily, and pushed his sword against Jack until the pirate's back was against the wall.

Jack swung the chain on his wrist around Will's sword and tried to pull it free. But Will was quick. He twisted the point of his sword through a link and stabbed it into the ceiling, leaving Jack hanging by his manacled wrist.

Jack kept fighting with one hand as he hung from the ceiling. He twisted around and compressed the furnace bellows with his foot. A shower of sparks flew into the air and hit Will in the face. Will stepped back and covered his eyes.

Jack used his full weight to yank the sword free from the ceiling. Then, dropping to the floor, he grabbed a mallet and hurled it at Will, smashing the boy's wrist. Will dropped his sword and fell. When he got up, Jack's pistol was aimed right between his eyes.

"You cheated!" Will shouted. Jack raised his eyebrows and smiled, as if to say, 'What do you expect from a pirate?'.

"You're lucky, boy," Jack told him, and motioned him away from the door. "This shot's not meant for you."

Jack was moving to make his escape when Mr Brown suddenly came out from a corner and slammed his bottle against Jack's skull.

Jack crumpled to the floor as the doors of the forge flew open and armed sailors rushed into the room. Commodore Norrington pushed his way to the front of the crowd. "Excellent work, Mr Brown," said Norrington, standing over Jack. "I believe you will always remember this as the day Captain Jack Sparrow *almost* escaped!"

As Norrington's men hauled Jack away, Mr Brown looked at the broken glass on the floor and sadly said, "That rotter broke my bottle!"

Chapter
6

Night fell, and the thick fog now blanketed the entire town of Port Royal. Only Fort Charles, high on a cliff, could be seen above the grey mist. But out in the harbour, cutting through the fog like a shark's fin, was the topmast of a tall, black ship flying the skull and crossbones. . . .

The fog brought a strange uneasiness with it. Elizabeth, cosy in her bed, was trying to read herself to sleep – but suddenly, the flame of her lamp flickered, then went out. She tried to turn it up, but it wouldn't work . . . the room was black.

In the blacksmith's shop, Will thought he heard a strange noise. He took an axe from the wall and stepped outside to look down the alley . . . but everything in the mist was still and silent.

Only Jack Sparrow, now stuck in a prison cell, had no fear of what might be lurking in the fog.

Jack's cell was next to that of three prisoners who were to be hanged along with him in the morning. The three had spent hours trying to coax a mangy dog with a ring of keys in its mouth over to their cell.

"You can keep doing that forever," Jack sighed as they waggled a bone at the dog. "That dog is never going to move."

"Excuse us if we ain't resigned ourselves to go to the gallows just yet," answered one of the prisoners, holding a loop of rope he hoped to land around the dog's neck. But Jack sat back and hoped for better things.

Commodore Norrington and Governor Swann were walking along the parapet overlooking the gallows when the sudden boom of cannon fire knocked them both off their feet. The explosion rocked the jail cell, too, sending Jack and his new-found friends running to the window. "I know those guns!" shouted Jack through the bars of his cell. "It's the *Black Pearl*!"

The fog lit up around the *Black Pearl* each time it fired its cannons on the town. Whole streets, buildings and docks exploded into bits. The citizens of Port Royal ran in horror. Then, out of the fog and smoke, came longboats loaded with pirates. Swarming ashore, the mob quickly overtook the town, running through the streets, setting fires and murdering any poor soul not quick enough to get away.

Will Turner armed himself with everything he could carry. He grabbed sabres, knives and a heavy broadaxe. The brash young blacksmith boldly headed up the street. A woman being chased by a pirate ran screaming past him. He backhanded the pirate square in the chest with the broad side of his axe and continued up the street.

Wiping dust and smoke from his eyes, Will looked up towards the governor's mansion. There, against the light of the moon, he saw the silhouettes of two pirates heading for the doors of the mansion. *Elizabeth!* he thought – but before he could act, pirates struck him from behind.

Chapter 7

A loud banging sent Elizabeth running to her window. She looked down and saw two brutes with their fists raised. She dashed from her room and reached the top of the mansion's staircase just as the butler opened the door. It was too late to warn him!

The two filthy pirates, one named Pintel and the other Ragetti, stormed into the room. The taller of the two, Ragetti, had a wooden eye that squeaked when it moved. They were each armed with a cutlass and pistol, shining and ready for use.

Elizabeth almost fainted when she heard the boom of the pirate's gun. The butler crumpled to the floor and the pirate holding the smoking pistol looked up at Elizabeth and smiled.

Terrified, Elizabeth ran to her room and locked the door as the two pirates charged up the stairs. Suddenly, a body slammed hard against the door, shaking it to its hinges. Elizabeth grabbed a bed warmer filled with hot coals and hit Pintel with it squarely in the face as he broke through the door. He staggered back, holding his burning, broken nose.

Elizabeth swung again as Ragetti rushed through the doorway. This time, the hot coals of the bed warmer spilled sizzling onto Ragetti's head, setting his hair and wooden eye on fire. Elizabeth ran for the hallway stairs.

The pirates burst from the bedroom, furious. They saw Elizabeth trying to escape down the stairs. In an instant, Ragetti vaulted over the banister to stop her. Behind her, Pintel was flying down the stairs. Ragetti landed in front of her, his hair and wooden eye still smouldering. She was trapped!

Suddenly, the wall of the mansion exploded as a cannonball ripped through the foyer. A chandelier came crashing to the floor, causing both pirates to take cover.

Elizabeth raced into the dining room and bolted the doors behind her. *If I could only find a weapon*, she thought as she frantically looked through the room. There was nothing. Knowing the pirates would break the doors down at any moment, she dived into a linen closet and hid.

Elizabeth held her breath, then cringed when she heard the pirates rush into the room. "We know you're here, poppet. Come out and we promise we won't hurt you," said Pintel, winking at his smouldering friend. "We will find you," he continued. "You've got something of ours, and it calls to us. The gold calls to us."

Elizabeth shrank back against the linen-laden shelves and looked down at the medallion around her neck. Light through a crack in the door glinted on the gold for an instant, then disappeared. Elizabeth looked up to see what was blocking the light and saw Pintel's eye glaring at her.

"Hello, poppet . . ."

Chapter
8

Ah, but it was shaping up to be a fine day, Jack Sparrow thought from his cell. The jail was being blown to bits around him, and with every boom of the *Black Pearl's* cannons, Jack knew he was that much closer to freedom.

But while cannonballs exploded throughout the prison, not one came through Jack's cell. "My sympathies, friend," said one of the prisoners from the next cell as the three made their escape through the rubble. "You've no manner of luck at all."

Jack had to agree as he watched them climb to the rocks below . . . and to freedom. He sat in his prison cell alone. The moon was just beginning to rise above the fog, and the *Black Pearl's* guns were firing in another direction.

Jack breathed a deep sigh, then looked around the battered prison and noticed the dog cowering under a long bench. The keys were still in its mouth. *What the heck*, thought Jack, and he reached into the next cell, picked up the old bone and said, "Here, doggie."

To his utter surprise, the dog got up! It moved closer and closer until the keys were almost in Jack's hand. But the dog became nervous. It started to whine, then stopped. "What's the matter, boy?" Jack asked. Just then the prison door slammed open and the dog bolted.

Two pirates from the *Black Pearl* swaggered in. "This isn't the armoury," one said to the other as they looked around. One of the pirates spotted Jack in the cell. "Well, well . . . look what we have here. It's Captain Sparrow."

"Last time we saw you, you were all alone on a godforsaken island," said the other. "How the devil did you get off . . . sprout little wings and fly?" The pirates laughed. "Your fortunes aren't improved much!"

"Worry about your own fortunes. The deepest circles of hell are for betrayers and mutineers!" snarled Jack fiercely. Not liking Jack's answer much, one of the pirates reached through the bars and grabbed him by the throat. Jack clutched at the pirate's arms and tried to wrestle free. But when he looked down, he saw that he wasn't holding arms at all. In the moonlight he saw nothing but the bare bones of a skeleton in his hands.

"There *is* a curse!" declared Jack, and the pirate snapped his hands back out of the light. Seeing the bones turn back to human flesh, Jack said, "So the stories *are* true!"

"You know nothing of hell," one of the pirates said. Then they turned their backs on him and walked out.

Chapter 9

Amid the thunder of cannon fire, a longboat piled high with loot slipped through the fog and out into the harbour. Elizabeth sat in the prow, terrified, as the pirates rowed the longboat towards the dark, massive hull of their ship.

As they rowed closer, Elizabeth could see on the bow an ornately carved figurehead of a woman with a small bird in her outstretched hand. Then she looked up as the fog parted. Looming high above her were yards and yards of black canvas. She was under the sails of the *Black Pearl*.

Smoke hung heavy on the lantern-lit deck as the longboat was raised to the rails. Elizabeth could see that the pirate crew had been mustered from many parts of the world. The heads of several were covered with knotted kerchiefs. Some wore silk waistcoats and ruffled capes, no doubt looted from some luckless ship that now sat wasted and rotting at the bottom of the sea. All were sunburned, savage men, and all had their eyes on Elizabeth!

"She's invoked the right of *parley* with Captain Barbossa," announced Pintel, pushing her onto the deck. The pirates were silent. Even cut-throats had a code of honour. The right of parley would protect any prisoner until he or she had had an audience with the captain.

Then, as if someone had spoken of the devil himself, the dark figure of a man slowly stepped out of the smoke and onto the main deck. It was the captain of the *Black Pearl* – Barbossa. A monkey jumped out of the rigging and landed on his shoulder, scaring Elizabeth senseless.

Barbossa stepped forward and Elizabeth tried to speak, but Bo'sun slapped her hard. "You'll speak when spoken to!" he hissed.

"And *you'll* not lay a hand on those under the protection of parley!" growled the captain, grabbing Bo'sun's wrist. "My apologies, miss," he said, turning to Elizabeth.

"I have come to negotiate the cessation of hostilities against Port Royal," she said, trying to appear confident.

Captain Barbossa smiled like the amused father of a small child. "There was a lot of long words in there, miss, and we're naught but humble pirates. What is it you want?"

"I want you to leave and never come back," Elizabeth answered firmly.

The crew laughed. Captain Barbossa told her that that would simply not be possible.

"Very well," said Elizabeth, running to the rail and dangling the gold medallion over the side. "I'll drop it!"

The crew suddenly went quiet. "I know it's what you're searching for," she said. "I recognize this ship. I saw it eight years ago."

"Did you, now?" said the captain, who didn't seem to care a rap about what Elizabeth had to say.

"Fine," said Elizabeth, flipping the medallion into the air. "Then there's no reason to keep it!"

The monkey screeched.

"No!" shouted Barbossa.

Elizabeth caught the medallion by its chain and smiled triumphantly.

Barbossa stepped back and took a long look at Elizabeth. "You have a name, missy?" he asked.

Elizabeth tried to think quickly. She was afraid things would be worse for her if they knew she was the governor's daughter, so she said, "Elizabeth. Elizabeth Turner." The pirates gave one another sidelong glances. "I'm a maid in the governor's household."

"Very well." Barbossa nodded. "Hand that over; we'll put your town to our rudder and ne'er return."

Elizabeth was thrilled that he would agree to leave. "Can I trust you?" she asked.

Captain Barbossa raised his voice and warned her, "Hand it over now, or these be the last friendly words you'll hear!"

Elizabeth had no choice. She held out the medallion. Bo'sun reached for it, but the monkey grabbed it first and took it to Barbossa.

"Our bargain?" asked Elizabeth anxiously.

Barbossa smiled and told Bo'sun to still the

guns. "Signal the men and make good to clear port."

Elizabeth was relieved to hear the cannon fire finally stop. Then she realized that the ship was leaving. "Wait!" she said. "You must return me to shore. According to the rules of order . . ."

Captain Barbossa wheeled around.

"First, your return to shore was not part of our negotiations nor our agreement, and so I must do nothing. Secondly, you must be a pirate for the pirates' code to apply. And thirdly," he said, smiling with teeth of gleaming gold and silver, "the code is more what you'd call guidelines than actual rules. Welcome aboard the *Black Pearl*, Miss Turner!"

Chapter
10

After the cannon fire stopped, the fog slowly lifted, revealing a harbour full of sunken and burning ships. Will Turner struggled to his feet and rubbed the bump on his head as he looked at the destruction. He thought only of Elizabeth as he raced to Fort Charles.

"They've taken her!" he shouted as he burst into Commodore Norrington's office.

Norrington and Governor Swann looked up for a moment from the map of the Caribbean draped over the desk; then Norrington turned to one of the two guards by the door. "Mr Murtogg, remove this man from my office."

Murtogg grabbed Will by the arm, but Will shook him off.

Norrington looked up impatiently. "Mr Turner, you are not a military man, you are not a sailor – you are a blacksmith. You have nothing of value to contribute here. And this is not a time for rash actions," he said.

"We have to hunt them down," Will protested, "and save her!"

"We'll launch a search mission on the next tide," Norrington said, looking back at his map.

Commodore Norrington and the governor were trying to calculate where the *Black Pearl* might be headed when Murtogg remembered something he'd heard: "That Jack Sparrow . . . he talked about the *Black Pearl*."

"Mentioned it, is more what he did," said the other guard.

"Ask him where it is!" demanded Will, knowing they were wasting precious time. "Make a deal with him! He can lead us to it!"

But Norrington refused. "Leave, Mr Turner!"

Will stormed out of the office and headed for the prison to speak to Jack Sparrow himself.

Jack was trying his luck at removing the bars of his cell when Will raced through the prison doors.

"You. Sparrow. Are you familiar with that ship . . . the *Black Pearl?*"

"Somewhat," answered Jack calmly.

"Where does it make berth?" Will demanded.

"The *Black Pearl* sails from the dreaded Isla de la Muerta. Surely you've heard the stories," answered Jack. "But why ask me?"

"They took Miss Swann," said Will, clenching his fists.

"Ah, so it *is* you found a girl," Jack said knowingly, ". . . but I see no profit in it for me."

Will pulled a bench up to Jack's cell. "I could get you out of here," he offered.

Jack looked into Will's face. "What's your name, boy?" he asked.

"Will Turner."

Jack smiled and nodded. "Well, Mr Turner, tell you what. I've changed my mind. You spring me from this cell, and I'll take you to the *Black Pearl*. Do we have an accord?" he asked, sticking his hand through the bars.

"Agreed!" said Will, and shook the pirate's hand firmly.

It was morning when Jack and Will made their way down to the dock. The *Dauntless* was still at anchor in the harbour.

"We're going to steal *that* ship?" asked Will, pointing to the *Dauntless*.

"Commandeer," said Jack, correcting him. "We're going to *commandeer* that ship . . . nautical term."

Jack led Will to an overturned rowing boat, and they both climbed under it. Jack instructed Will to raise the rowing boat to shoulder height. Then the two began walking toward the water, zigzagging along the beach like a crab.

"This is either brilliant or crazy," Will said as they walked into the water.

"Remarkable how often those two traits coincide," answered Jack.

They had tied bags of sand around the rowing boat for ballast. Safely breathing the air that was trapped in the rowing boat's hull, the two men moved closer and closer to the ship.

The racket of sailors aboard ship went silent when Jack and Will suddenly jumped over the rail of the *Dauntless*. "Everybody stay calm," announced Jack, brandishing a pistol. "We're taking over the ship!"

The crew looked at Jack, then at Will – and burst out laughing. "This ship cannot be crewed by two men!" said one of the sailors. "You'll never make it out of the bay!"

But the prediction didn't worry Jack. "I've never been one to resist a challenge," he said, motioning with his pistol for the crew to climb into the rowing boat.

In the meantime, aboard Norrington's ship, the *Interceptor*, the crew was setting up the rigging. The commodore was readying to make sail and hunt down the *Black Pearl*. From the *Interceptor*'s deck, Norrington noticed that the *Dauntless* seemed to be moving. He took out his spyglass for a closer look. Sure enough, it was sailing out of the harbour! He then recognized Will on the main deck and Jack Sparrow at the wheel – the *Dauntless* was now theirs!

Chapter
11

Norrington couldn't believe his eyes! Jack Sparrow was trying to commandeer the *Dauntless*! Norrington knew that the *Interceptor* was faster than the *Dauntless*, and with only Jack and Will to sail the *Dauntless*, he'd catch them in no time! He gave his crew the order and they took off full sail.

"Here they come!" Will shouted to Jack.

As the *Interceptor* drew up alongside its quarry, Norrington found the decks of the *Dauntless* empty. "Search every cabin, every hold, down to the bilges!" he commanded as the entire crew of the *Interceptor* boarded the *Dauntless*.

But that left the *Interceptor* empty except for one lone sentry. In a flash, Jack and Will climbed over the rail unseen. The *Interceptor* was theirs!

"Can you swim?" Jack asked the sentry, grabbing the man's neck.

"Like a fish . . ." the sentry promised.

"Good," said Jack, and threw him overboard.

Jack and Will quickly threw off the ropes that held the two ships together and raised the foresail.

Seeing the *Interceptor* move away, Norrington shouted to his crew to turn the *Dauntless* and man the cannons. But it was too late. Jack had cut the rudder chain of the *Dauntless*, leaving it in his wake. The *Interceptor* was sailing into the horizon to find the *Black Pearl*, with Jack Sparrow at the wheel.

Locked in a cabin aboard the *Black Pearl*, Elizabeth was startled when two pirates barged through the door. They were the same two who had taken her from the mansion, Pintel and his one-eyed friend, Ragetti.

"You'll be dining with the captain. He requests you wear this," said Pintel, shoving a black silk dress toward her. The two turned and left Elizabeth to change. She was examining the dress when she heard a loud squeak coming from the door. The pirates were peeking through the keyhole!

Elizabeth took a hairpin, pushed it through the keyhole, and felt it hit something hard and wooden. "*Ow!* Me eye!" howled Ragetti. The hairpin plucked the wooden eye from his head and sent it rolling down the deck.

"Don't let it drown!" he yelled, and went scrambling after it. The eye rolled to a stop under the boot of Bo'sun, who said, "I'd be happy to nail it in place for ya!" and kicked it down the deck. Every pirate aboard roared with laughter as they stomped past the one-eyed pirate, who was now bumping around the deck on his hands and knees.

In Captain Barbossa's cabin, a huge feast was laid out on the table. Elizabeth wore the black silk dress and watched Captain Barbossa enter the cabin with the monkey on his shoulder.

"You must be hungry," he told her, motioning to the meat and bread on the table. "Please . . . dig in."

Elizabeth was starving. She tore off a large piece of bread and took a bite. "Try the wine," the captain said with fierce delight, "and the apples . . . one of those next."

Elizabeth stopped for a second and realized the captain was watching her put the food into her mouth and chew – so were all the pirates . . . so was the monkey!

Thinking the food was poisoned, Elizabeth panicked.

"You eat it!" she cried.

"Would that I could," replied the captain, looking at the feast in front of him. He knew there wasn't a man on board who could take a bite and taste it. He took the gold medallion from his pocket and dangled it from his finger.

"This is Aztec gold," he said, falling into a sombre mood. "One of 882 identical pieces delivered in a stone chest to Cortés himself. Blood money, Miss Turner. . . . And so the heathen gods placed upon the gold a terrible curse."

"I hardly believe in ghost stories," Elizabeth said.

Captain Barbossa shook his head. "Aye, that's exactly what I thought when first we were told the tale!

"Buried on an Island of the Dead," Barbossa recalled, "find it we did. And there be the chest, and inside be the coins . . . and we took 'em all. Spent 'em and traded 'em for drink and food and pleasant company. But the more we gave 'em away, the more we came to realize: the drink would not satisfy, and the food turned to ash in our mouths. We are cursed men, Miss Turner. Compelled by greed we were, but now we are consumed by it."

Barbossa placed a consoling hand on the monkey, which whimpered as his master told the tale.

"But there is one way to end the curse," Barbossa said, raising an eyebrow. "All the scattered pieces of the Aztec gold must be restored . . . and the blood repaid.

"Ten years we searched, looting ship and port, sifting through our plunder for it all!" He looked at the medallion lovingly. "And now, thanks to you, we have the final piece. Once we've reunited it with its mates, we are free."

Elizabeth thought for a moment. "And the blood to be repaid?" she asked. "What of it?"

Barbossa looked at her and smiled. "Apple?" he asked her. Elizabeth was stunned. She suddenly realized that it was her blood he wanted.

Horrified, Elizabeth bolted out of her chair. She struggled for a moment with Captain Barbossa, then reached for a table knife and plunged it into his chest. The captain calmly looked at the wound, and to Elizabeth's shock, no blood came from it.

Terrified, Elizabeth ran from the cabin to the deck of the ship. There in the moonlight she saw the crew of the *Black Pearl* at work and froze. She shut her eyes tightly.

Captain Barbossa came up on deck and grabbed her. "Look!" he shouted. "The moonlight shows us for what we really are!"

Elizabeth opened her eyes and saw the pirates

at their stations, coiling the lines and raising the black sails. They sang an old sea shanty as they worked, but where the moonlight fell across their bodies, Elizabeth saw nothing but the bones of skeletons!

The skeletal monkey, holding the medallion, shrieked and jumped onto Captain Barbossa's shoulder. "We are not among the living," Barbossa said as two skeletons played a pirate tune, "and so we cannot die!" He leaned into the moonlight, turning his face into a fleshless skull.

The captain took a bottle of wine from an open case by the cabin door and uncorked it with his teeth. He raised it as if in a toast to Elizabeth.

"You'd best start believing in ghost stories, Miss Turner," Barbossa advised as he drank straight from the bottle, the wine gushing out from between his empty ribs. "You're in one."

Chapter 12

The *Interceptor* was as fast as Jack had hoped, and with a favouring wind it could log a fair distance in a day's run. Jack reckoned they were now only a few miles from Tortuga, where he knew he could find himself an able crew.

Jack was surprised at how quickly Will had taken to being a sailor. "I worked passage from England as a cabin boy," Will explained. "After my mother passed, I came out here looking for my father . . . Bill Turner."

"That so?" asked Jack slyly.

"You knew my father," Will said to Jack. "It was only after you learned my name at the jail that you agreed to help."

Jack sighed and considered what story he might tell Will, but then decided to tell him the truth. "I knew him," he said. "Most everyone just called him Bill . . . Bootstrap Bill."

"Bootstrap?" said Will, surprised.

"Good man," answered Jack. "Good pirate."

Will looked shocked. "It's not true that my father was a pirate!" he declared. "He was a merchant marine! A respectable man who obeyed the law!"

"Ah, there's quite a few who come out here hoping to amass enough swag to ease the burdens of respectable life . . . and they're all merchant marines," said Jack with a knowing smile.

"My father did not think of his family as a burden!" argued Will.

"Sure, because he could always go pirating!" Jack said.

"My father was not a pirate!" exclaimed Will, pulling out his sword.

"Put it away," Jack said to Will in a dull voice. "It's not worth getting beat again." When Jack saw that Will was going to push the point, he turned the wheel of the *Interceptor* hard, and the boom whipped around and struck Will in the chest.

Will held on as the boom carried him out over the foaming sea. "As long as you're just hanging there," said Jack, picking up Will's sword, "pay attention. You can accept that your father was a pirate and still a good man – or you can't. Now me, I can let you drown . . . but I can't land this ship at Tortuga without your help."

A wave came up and almost cost Will his grip. "So . . . " Jack said, pointing the sword at Will, "can you sail under the command of a pirate or not?"

With the island of Tortuga lying dead ahead and Jack's sword pointing at him, Will agreed. Jack swung the boom around, and Will set his feet back on the deck. Then Jack handed him his sword and smiled.

Together, they trimmed the forward jib and readied the mooring lines. The *Interceptor* would soon arrive in Tortuga.

Chapter
13

Jack stepped ashore, happy to be in a port that felt like home. A woman with red hair and a redder dress walked up to Jack. "Scarlett!" exclaimed Jack, putting out his arms. She slapped his face and stalked off.

"I didn't deserve that," said Jack. Will raised an eyebrow but didn't say a word.

Tortuga was a dank, dirty port where the tides had swept together the scum of the Caribbean, and Jack Sparrow loved it all. He could hear the laughter of drunken pirates as they chased women through the streets and dunked a merchant just for sport.

"What do you think?" Jack asked as a woman

dumped a chamber pot from a window above them.

"It'll linger," answered Will, turning his head to avoid the stench.

"Aye, unforgettable," agreed Jack, not noticing Will's distaste. "I tell you, Will, if every town in the world was like this one, no man would ever feel unwanted!"

A blonde young lady stepped up to Jack. "Giselle!" exclaimed Jack with a smile. She smiled back, slapped him hard and walked on.

"I didn't deserve that, either," said Jack, rubbing his face.

"How many women are there in this town?" asked Will, worrying for Jack's future.

"You're right," said Jack after a moment's thought. "The quicker we get our crew and away, the better! And here's where we'll find our quartermaster," he said, pointing to a tavern called The Faithful Bride.

Will looked up at a hanging sign that showed a bride holding a bouquet of flowers, her wrists manacled and chained. "This way!" said Jack, leading Will around to the back of the tavern.

Lying in the mud with two pigs behind the tavern was old Joshaemee Gibbs. *Drunk, as usual,* thought Jack as he threw a bucket of water over Gibbs's face.

"Curse you for breathing!" sputtered Gibbs – then he opened his eyes and saw Jack's face.

Jack was helping his old friend to his feet when Will doused the man with another bucket of water. "Blast it, I'm already awake!" Gibbs yelled.

"That was for the smell," Will said as Jack helped Gibbs stumble into the tavern.

Jack and Gibbs sat in a dark corner of The Faithful Bride while Will kept a lookout at the door. Their table was lit by a single candle, and they leaned in close so as not to be heard. "I'm going after the *Black Pearl*," whispered Jack. Gibbs straightened up.

"It's a fool's errand," he told Jack. "Why, you know better than me the tales of the *Black Pearl!*"

"Then it's a good thing I'm not a fool," replied Jack, raising his glass with a grin.

Gibbs was not convinced. "Prove me wrong," he said. "What makes you think Barbossa will give

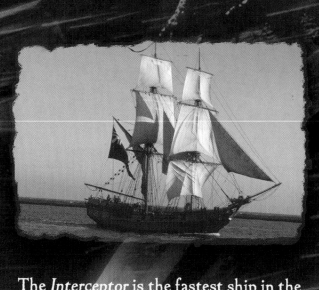

The *Interceptor* is the fastest ship in the
Caribbean Sea and the pride of Port Royal.

Young Elizabeth Swann watches over Will Turner.

Commodore Norrington vows to rid the sea of pirates.

Elizabeth's father wants her to marry Norrington,
but she wants nothing to do with the rigid commodore.

Swashbuckler Jack Sparrow plots to get his ship, the *Black Pearl*, back from Captain Barbossa.

The evil pirate Barbossa finally finds the last piece of cursed gold.

Jack and Will Turner take possession of the *Interceptor* to save Elizabeth from Barbossa and his pirate crew.

Barbossa tells Elizabeth how he plans to lift the curse from his crew . . . with her blood!

The gold is returned – but Barbossa
and his crew are still cursed!

As a joke, the pirates name their mean
little monkey Jack after Jack Sparrow.

The bumbling pirates Pintel and Ragetti
never get anything right.

Free of Barbossa and his crew, Will and Jack
take command of the *Black Pearl* once more.

Elizabeth and Will watch as Norrington
gives the order to hang Jack for piracy.

Everyone watches as Jack Sparrow
makes yet another daring escape.

Elizabeth and Will finally kiss . . . and they
live happily ever after.

up the *Black Pearl* to you?"

"I've got the right leverage," Jack answered, jerking his head toward Will, who stood at the door out of earshot.

"The kid?"

"That is the child of Bootstrap Bill Turner. His *only* child!" whispered Jack.

Gibbs looked over at Will, who was trying to keep some scoundrel from chasing a serving wench, then narrowed his eyes. "Leverage, say you. I think I feel a change in the wind,' says I. I'll find us a crew!" he said excitedly, and slammed his tankard down on the table.

By morning, Gibbs had lined up every weather-beaten, ragged rogue in Tortuga for Jack's inspection. "Feast your eyes, Cap'n. All of them faithful hands before the mast. Every man worth his salt, and crazy to boot!"

Jack moved down the line. It was a motley crew of men, some of whom looked like they hadn't seen a patch of good luck in a good, long time. He passed several, then came upon a bright-eyed prospect with a large, colourful parrot on his shoulder. Jack looked at him and raised an eyebrow . . . but the sailor said nothing.

"Cotton here is mute, sir. Poor devil had his tongue cut out," said Gibbs, opening up Cotton's mouth. Jack cringed. "So he went and trained the parrot to talk for him," Gibbs continued brightly.

"Wind in your sails!" screeched the parrot.

Jack sighed, nodded, and continued on. He stopped in front of a hunched sailor whose face was shaded by a three-cornered hat. Jack leaned over to get a closer look and was suddenly slapped to the ground. The hat fell away and there stood a woman as strong and tall as Jack.

"Guess you didn't deserve that one, either?" asked Will.

"No, that one I deserved," answered Jack. "Hello, AnaMaria."

"You stole my boat!" she shouted.

"Borrowed," said Jack. "Without permission – but with every intention of bringing it back!"

"And did you bring it back?" AnaMaria demanded.

"Ah . . . no, but I've got something better," answered Jack, motioning to the *Interceptor*.

Jack looked at the line of men. "I'm asking all of you to join my crew," he announced. "Sail under my command, and at voyage's end, the *Interceptor* will be yours! What do you say?"

The sailors nodded enthusiastically. "Aye! I'm in!" they shouted.

"You can get your assignments from my first mate," Jack said, and nodded to AnaMaria. "Prepare to set sail!"

The crew poured onto the *Interceptor* immediately and the ship left Tortuga within the hour.

Chapter 14

Far out over the Caribbean Sea, thunder cracked. The *Interceptor* pitched from side to side as it headed into the dark clouds of a great storm. Jack stood at the ship's bow, looked at his compass and nodded. Things were going well, he thought. Again he looked at his compass, which never pointed to true north but always pointed the way to Isla de la Muerta, berth of the *Black Pearl*.

The ship tilted in the high seas and howling wind, the white canvas of its sails stretched tight.

"We'd best drop the canvas, sir!" shouted Gibbs, fearing that the sails might come apart.

"She can hold a bit longer," answered Jack as

the storm gained force. The wind picked up speed, roaring through the ship. Jack looked at his compass, then out to sea. He smiled.

"What's in your head as puts you in such a fine mood, Captain?" shouted Gibbs over the wind.

"We're catching up!" answered Jack.

In the meantime, on the deck of the *Black Pearl*, Elizabeth was being bound and gagged by Pintel.

"Time to go, poppet," he said with a smirk, yanking the ropes at her wrist. She tried to jerk away as Captain Barbossa was draping the gold medallion around her neck, but it did her no good. He tilted her head to judge the look of it and smiled.

Elizabeth was placed in a longboat laden with treasure, one of several that began to row from the *Black Pearl*. As they passed out of the fog, Elizabeth could see a dark sea cave looming ahead. The longboats glided into the cave and were swallowed by the darkness. They had arrived on the dreaded Isla de la Muerta.

Chapter 15

"Dead men tell no tales!" squawked Cotton's parrot as the *Interceptor* slowly slipped into the fog surrounding the island. The crew was watchful and tense.

Suddenly, as the ship emerged from the dense fog, there came a low scraping sound from below. Will looked around to find that they had sailed into a graveyard of the many ships that had been dashed on the reefs surrounding Isla de la Muerta. It was the mast of one such ship that now scraped the bottom of the *Interceptor* and threatened to take her under.

Jack was at the wheel. He quickly snapped his compass shut and concentrated on navigating through the graveyard. He made a few small corrections and the scraping stopped. Gibbs and Will stared at the grey bones of the dead ships as the *Interceptor* slowly glided past.

"Where'd he get that compass?" Will whispered.

"Told me once he served as apprentice to a cartographer for a time," Gibbs answered. "But I can't say . . . only heard he showed up in Tortuga one night with a notion to go for the treasure of Isla de la Muerta. This was when he was captain of the *Black Pearl*."

"What?" said Will, surprised to hear that the *Black Pearl* had once belonged to Jack Sparrow.

Will leaned in closer to hear the tale. "Ah, but Jack Sparrow has an honest streak in him. That's where all his problems start," Gibbs lamented.

Gibbs explained that Jack had promised each member of the crew an equal share of treasure. Shaking his head, Gibbs said, "So his first mate come to him and says if everything's an equal share, that should mean the location of the treasure, too. So Jack gave up the bearings.

"That night, there was mutiny," Gibbs said sadly. "They marooned Jack on an island and left him there to die.

"Now, when a pirate's marooned, he's given a pistol with a single shot. After three weeks of a starving belly and thirst, that pistol starts to look real friendly," Gibbs said, putting his finger to his head to demonstrate for Will.

"But Jack – he survived!" exclaimed Gibbs. "And he still has that single shot. He won't use it, though, save on one man. His mutinous first mate . . ."

"Barbossa!" said Will, seeing the pieces fall into place.

"Aye."

"But how did Jack get off the island?" asked Will.

"He roped himself some sea turtles, lashed 'em together, and made a raft," said the old sailor with a firm nod.

"Sea turtles?" asked Will, unbelieving.

"Aye," Gibbs said earnestly; then Jack suddenly ordered his crew to drop anchor and lower the rowing boat.

"Will and I are going ashore," he announced.

"Aye, Captain," answered AnaMaria.

Gibbs leaned in close to Jack. "And if the worst should happen?" he asked quietly.

"Keep to the code," answered Jack. "You know that."

Chapter
16

Jack and Will rowed into the still waters of the cave, where the air was moist and thick. On the wall hung a lantern, and to one side, Will could see the skeleton of a man half buried in the sand, a sword still stuck in his back.

As they drifted past the poor blighter, Will asked Jack a question. "What code is Gibbs to keep to, if the worst should happen?"

Jack kept rowing. "Pirates' code," he said. "Any man who falls behind is left behind."

Suddenly, several small bright circles began to shimmer on the wall of the cave, then dozens more. Will looked around but couldn't find the source. Then he glanced down into the water and saw thousands of gold coins reflecting the light from the lantern: all of it treasure that had been spilled from the many trips Barbossa and his pirates had made into the cave.

Will and Jack silently rowed to a landing where the pirates had moored their longboats. Will pulled the boat ashore. Jack hopped out and led Will up a short slope.

Carefully, they looked over the top into a vast cavern. Will couldn't believe what he saw. The entire cavern was filled with the most spectacular treasure.

Glittering in the pirates' torchlight were bars of silver; gold boxes set with diamonds; rings with sparkling jewels; rubies large and small; great, long strings of pearls; brightly coloured silks; and piles of gold dust and coins. At the centre of the cave, the pirates emptied trunks of gold and silver around Elizabeth, who stood bound next to an Aztec stone chest.

Will tried to scramble over the top of the rise to save her, but Jack held him back. "We wait for the opportune moment!" he whispered.

But Will was in no mood to wait. Elizabeth's

life was at stake. "Sorry, Jack . . . but I'm not going to be your leverage," he said, and brought an oar down over Jack's head. The monkey suddenly looked up, but then swivelled his little head around when Captain Barbossa began to speak.

"You know the first thing I'm going to do after this curse is lifted?" he asked, grinning at Elizabeth. "Eat a whole bushel of apples!" The pirates laughed as Barbossa raised his knife and sliced the middle of Elizabeth's palm. He placed the medallion in her hand and closed her fist around it.

Barbossa took the bloody medallion from her and dropped it into the stone chest. "Begun by blood, by blood undone!" he shouted.

The pirates tensed, waiting to see what would happen when the curse was finally lifted. "I don't feel no different," said the one-eyed pirate after a time. The men looked at one another. "How do we tell?" Pintel asked.

Barbossa frowned, took out his pistol, and shot Pintel in the chest! The crew was completely disappointed when Pintel didn't fall down dead.

"It didn't work!" they complained. "The curse is still upon us!"

Barbossa was furious. He turned to Elizabeth and grabbed her. "You. Was your father William Turner?"

"No," gulped Elizabeth.

The pirates were in an uproar and began to shout. "You two," yelled Bo'sun, pointing at Pintel and his one-eyed friend, "you brought us the wrong person!"

"But she had the medallion, and she's the proper age!" the one-eyed pirate pleaded.

Then Bo'sun turned to Barbossa. "It's you who sent Bootstrap to the depths."

"Aye, it's you what brought us here in the first place!" yelled another. The shouting became louder, and soon every pirate was on his feet.

"I say we cut her neck and spill all her blood, just in case . . . " shouted Bo'sun.

Suddenly, Elizabeth felt a hand over her mouth. It was Will. In all the fighting, no one noticed Will untying Elizabeth. The two crouched down and headed for the water. But before they slipped away, Elizabeth grabbed the medallion.

The monkey saw it all. His screeching echoed through the cavern as he pointed towards Will and Elizabeth. Barbossa looked around and threw up his arms. "They've taken the medallion!" he yelled. "After them! Fetch it back!"

The pirates raced to their longboats, but the oars were missing! "Find 'em!" yelled Bo'sun.

Into the middle of the confusion walked Jack Sparrow, dazed from the whack on the head he'd received from Will.

"You!" said Ragetti, recognizing Jack. "You're supposed to be dead!"

"I'm not?" asked Jack, staggering around the treasure.

The pirates drew their swords and pistols and Jack came to his senses. "Parley," he said.

The pirates lowered their weapons. Pintel threw his to the ground. "Parley?" Pintel shouted. "Curses to whatever muttonhead ever thought up parley!"

Captain Barbossa stepped forward and stared at Jack. "Kill him," he said, and turned away.

Pintel happily raised his gun and was aiming

when Jack said to Barbossa, "The girl's blood didn't work, did it?"

Barbossa snapped back around. "Hold fire," he told Pintel, who was now truly disappointed.

"I know whose blood you need," Jack said.

Chapter
17

Will threw the last of the pirates' oars over the side, then helped Elizabeth board the *Interceptor*. "Jack ain't with you?" asked Gibbs.

"Where be Jack, boy?" asked AnaMaria sternly.

Elizabeth gasped. She realized that she had been saved not only by Will – but also by the notorious pirate, Jack Sparrow.

"Fell behind," Will answered AnaMaria. Then he moved away to tend to Elizabeth. Gibbs and AnaMaria exchanged a grim glance.

"Weigh anchor and hoist the sails," AnaMaria ordered the crew, and the *Interceptor* headed out for the open sea.

Below decks, Will took out some bandages for the cut on Elizabeth's hand. As he tenderly tied the bandages around her wound, they looked into each other's eyes. Will leaned in to kiss her, but Elizabeth took his hand instead. She placed the medallion from her neck into Will's palm. "This is yours," she told him. Will looked at it, confused.

"Don't you recognize it?" she asked.

"I thought I'd lost it," answered Will. "It was a gift from my father."

Will stared at the medallion. "This is part of the treasure . . ." he said, then realized, ". . . it was *my* blood they needed. My father's blood. The blood of a pirate."

On board the *Black Pearl*, Jack roamed the cabin and examined the sorry state it was in. Captain Barbossa sat behind his desk and glowered at the man he so hated.

"I'm disappointed, Barbossa," Jack said, polishing a bit of brass with the back of his sleeve. "I expected you to take better care of my ship."

"It's not your ship," snapped Barbossa.

"The very issue we need to rectify," said Jack.

"That's the terms you're negotiating for?" asked Barbossa. "You get the *Black Pearl*? You expect to leave me standing on some beach with nothing more than a name and your word it's the one we need, and then watch you sail away on my ship?"

Jack sat down and put his feet on the desk. "Oh, no, I expect to leave you standing on some beach watching me sail away on *my* ship, and then I'll shout the name back to you!"

Jack picked up an apple and took a bite. Barbossa watched him savour the taste. "I suppose I should thank you," Jack said. "If you hadn't betrayed me and left me to die, I'd have had an equal share in the curse, same as you! Funny old world," mused Jack, enjoying his apple.

But he changed his tune when Bo'sun suddenly appeared at the cabin door. "Captain, we're coming up on the *Interceptor*," he said.

Jack quickly followed Barbossa to the deck. He worried things wouldn't go well for the *Interceptor* if it had to come up against the *Black Pearl*.

"What do you say to this?" Jack offered. "I'll go aboard and negotiate with them, get you your medallion back, and there'll be no need to swab blood off the decks later."

Barbossa shook his head. "Now, see, Jack. That's exactly the attitude that lost you the *Pearl*!

"Lock him in the brig!" he said flatly.

Barbossa took the wheel of the *Black Pearl* in his hands. "Raise the sails and run out the guns!" he shouted to his crew. "Haul on the mainsails and let go!"

The small hatches on the side of the *Black Pearl* opened, and large galley oars extended from each side of the ship. The pirates rowed in unison, and the *Black Pearl* moved faster and faster. Behind Captain Barbossa, the crew hoisted the skull and crossbones of the Jolly Roger!

On the deck of the *Interceptor*, Gibbs could see the *Black Pearl* gaining on them. "Shake out the sails!" he shouted. "I want to see every inch of canvas we've got!"

"What's happening?" Elizabeth asked when she heard the commotion on deck. Then she saw the *Black Pearl* on the horizon.

"Lighten the ship!" shouted AnaMaria in

hopes of getting the *Interceptor* to pick up some speed and outrun the *Black Pearl*. "Anything we can afford to lose, see it's lost!"

From the deck, the crew threw crates, barrels, and cannonballs over the side. But the *Black Pearl* was gaining fast. It was almost on them! "We're going to have to fight!" shouted AnaMaria. "Load the guns!"

"*Uh-oh!*" squawked Cotton's parrot. The cannonballs were already over the side, so the crew loaded everything they could find into the guns: silverware, nails, even crushed glass!

Barbossa knew the *Interceptor* would never get a shot off unless the *Black Pearl* came up alongside, so he stayed to its stern.

Elizabeth saw the problem and had an idea. "Drop the anchor!" she shouted to AnaMaria.

"You're daft!" AnaMaria shouted back, but Gibbs got the idea.

"Do it!" he yelled to the crew. "Or it's you we'll be loading into the cannons!"

The anchor splashed into the water, hit the bottom and caught on the reef. The anchor line went taut and the *Interceptor* heaved as it pivoted in a circle, bringing it broadside to the *Black Pearl*.

"Fire all!" shouted AnaMaria.

Barbossa raised his cutlass and cried out for more cannon fire. The two ships opened fire!

On the gun deck of the *Black Pearl*, Pintel looked over to see a spoon embedded in a post beside his head. Then he saw Ragetti with a fork stuck in that blasted wooden eye! He yanked on the fork and managed to pull the eye out with it. The two looked at each other and shook their heads.

Below decks, the door of the brig was blown off by a blast of cannon. "Stop putting holes in my ship!" shouted Jack as he pushed through the door. "That's it, I'm putting an end to this," he huffed, coming up on the *Black Pearl*'s deck.

Barbossa ordered a second round of fire on the *Interceptor*. The blast shattered the ship's mainmast. The mast leaned, then came crashing down across the *Black Pearl*, smashing the deck next to Barbossa.

He didn't flinch. "Find me that medallion!" he

shouted to his crew. The monkey scampered across the fallen mast, followed by a swarm of pirates swinging from the rigging.

One pirate missed his landing and swung backwards. Jack intercepted the line with a thank-you salute to the pirate as he splashed into the sea.

Jack leaped out on the line as the two crews battled on the decks below him. Then he saw Gibbs with pirates coming at him from both sides. Jack swung down and hit the first one hard, then swung back and got the second. "Jack, you're alive!" Gibbs shouted to his old friend as Jack dropped onto the main deck.

Chapter 18

Below the deck of the *Interceptor*, the blast of a cannon had knocked a beam across the door of Will's cabin. The water was rising fast, and Will couldn't get the door to budge. He was pulling with all his might when a screech turned his head. It was the cursed monkey. The monkey grabbed the medallion and made his way back out through a hole in the bulkhead.

The water was almost to the top of the cabin. Desperate, Will took a breath and went under.

On the deck, the monkey raced past Jack, who saw that the animal had the medallion. Jack chased him across the broken mast back to the *Black Pearl*. He was about to snatch the medallion from the monkey's nasty little paw when a hand reached down and grabbed it.

"Why, thank you, Jack," Barbossa said with an unpleasant grin.

"You're welcome," Jack replied grimly.

"Not you," Barbossa said. "We named the monkey Jack."

It seemed that all was lost. Barbossa's pirates had overtaken the *Interceptor*, and it was sinking fast. Gibbs finally signalled their surrender as Barbossa raised the medallion. "The prize is ours!" he shouted to his cheering pirates.

Jack's crew was roughly taken aboard the *Black Pearl* and tied to the mast by Pintel and Ragetti.

"Any of you so much as thinks the word 'parley', I'll have your guts for garters!" Pintel said, holding his pistol on them.

Suddenly, a huge explosion came from the battered *Interceptor*, the debris landing on the *Black Pearl*'s deck.

There, standing on the rail and soaking wet, was Will, alive and well and pointing a pistol at

Barbossa's head. "She goes free!" he demanded.

"What's in your head, boy? You've got one shot . . . and we can't die."

"You can't. I can," said Will, putting the gun's muzzle under his chin. "My name is Will Turner," he announced. "My father was Bootstrap Bill Turner. His blood runs in my veins!"

Every pirate on deck looked at Will in surprise, but Jack only shook his head in dismay.

"Why, it's the spittin' image of old Bootstrap, come back to haunt us!" said Ragetti.

"And on my word," said Will as he cocked the trigger, "do as I say, or I will pull the trigger and sink all the way down to Davy Jones's locker!"

"Name your terms, Mr Turner," said Barbossa flatly. He knew that if Will pulled the trigger, they'd be cursed forever.

"Elizabeth goes free!" Will answered.

"Yes, we know that one," said Barbossa. "Anything else?"

Will hadn't thought that far ahead. "And Jack," he finally added. "He goes free, too. And the crew . . . they're not to be harmed! Agree!" he demanded as he leaned out over the water.

"Agreed," Barbossa said. "You have my word as a gentleman of fortune."

"You can't trust him!" Elizabeth shouted.

"You can trust this," Barbossa hissed, grinding his teeth. "Pull that trigger and the girl will be the first to suffer – and the last to die!"

Will slowly lowered his gun. Pirates immediately swarmed him. Fearing what might happen next, Jack stepped up to Barbossa. "What about our bargain?" he demanded.

"I've got the *Pearl*, and I've got the child of Bootstrap Bill now. And you've got–" he glared hard at Jack "–nothing to bargain with.

"But no worries, Jack. See that island over there?" Barbossa asked, pointing to a patch of sea-washed sand. "If memory serves, it be the same one we made you governor of on our last trip. I'll wager that by whatever miracle you escaped before, you won't be able to conjure it again. For you or the girl!"

"You swore they'd go free!" Will protested.

"Aye, so I did . . . and so they will," agreed Barbossa. "But you never made specific mention of when, nor where."

Will struggled furiously against the pirates who now held him back.

"Men!" Barbossa shouted to his crew. "The plank!"

Chapter
19

A shark's fin glided past the *Black Pearl* as Jack, hands tied behind his back, stood on the plank. "Last time you left me a pistol with one shot," he said before taking the step that would land him in the company of the sharks below.

"By the powers, you're right!" said Barbossa, enjoying the moment. "Where's Jack's pistol?" he asked the crew. "Bring it forward!"

"Seeing that there's two of us," Jack said, nodding at Elizabeth, "a gentleman would give us two pistols."

"It'll be one pistol, as before," Barbossa answered, taking Jack's pistol from one of the pirates, "and *you* can be the gentleman, an' shoot the lady, and starve to death yourself!"

The pirates hooted with laughter as Barbossa took Jack's gun and tossed it over the side.

Jack suddenly felt the point of a cutlass at his back and stumbled off the edge of the plank. He plunged straight down into the water.

"The lady's next!" declared Barbossa.

The pirates took her by both arms. Elizabeth remained calm. She showed the pirates no fear as she stepped onto the plank. She turned once and looked back at Will. She was about to say something to him when Bo'sun shook the plank and she tumbled off the end.

Bubbles foamed around Elizabeth as she plunged into the sea. She opened her eyes underwater and saw fish scatter in all directions. Then she looked up and saw the circling sharks—hammerheads, their dark shapes gliding through the warm turquoise water.

She held her breath, turning her head and looking for Jack. She saw him swimming towards the bottom, his hands still tied behind his back. She dived down, grabbed at the ropes and untied him.

Jack immediately swam to the bottom, ran his hands through the sand, and found the pistol.

Elizabeth began to swim for the surface, but Jack grabbed her ankle and jerked her back down. She struggled, then looked at Jack, who was shaking his head, pointing up at the sharks.

Jack forced Elizabeth to swim along the bottom with him until they reached the reef. Finally, they both surfaced, choking and gasping for air.

"Why?" coughed Elizabeth, not understanding why Jack had held her under.

"Sharks attack from below," he said, breathing hard. She nodded grimly.

Jack turned and looked out to sea. The *Black Pearl* was quickly moving away under full sail. "That's the second time I've had to watch that man sail away with my ship!" he said angrily.

Jack and Elizabeth swam the little bit of sea that separated the reef from the island.

"Not all that big, is it?" commented Elizabeth when they got to shore. Jack didn't seem to be bothered by the size of the island. He'd been marooned and left to die on it before.

As Elizabeth walked the shore, Jack took apart his pistol and laid it out on his bandana. When it was dry, he reassembled it and began digging a deep hole.

"What are you doing?" Elizabeth asked him.

Jack grabbed hold of a large iron ring at the bottom of the hole and began to pull.

"Is there a boat under there?" she asked excitedly. "Is that how you escaped the last time?"

"In a way . . ." answered Jack as he heaved a trap door open, revealing a deep, dark pit. Inside, he could see barrels of rum covered with dust and cobwebs.

Elizabeth looked at the barrels. "How will this help us get away?" she asked.

"It won't," sighed Jack, jumping into the pit and opening a bottle of rum, "and so we won't."

"But you did it before!"

"Last time," explained Jack as he took a swig of the rum, "I was here for a grand total of three days. Last time, the rum-runners who used this island as a hiding place came by, and I bartered passage off. But from the looks here," he said, running his hand through the cobwebs, "they've long been taken out of business." He took another swig of rum, then added, "We probably have your friend Norrington to credit for that."

Elizabeth was shocked. "So that's it?" she asked, hoping for a better explanation. "You spent three days lying on the beach drinking rum?"

"Welcome to the Caribbean, love," sighed Jack as he gathered a few bottles and headed for the beach.

"You should look at it this way," he told her as he began to build a fire. "We've got some food on the trees. And we've got rum. We can stay alive a month, maybe more."

"A month?" exclaimed Elizabeth. "Will doesn't have a month! We have to do something now!"

"Ah, you're right," Jack answered, and raised his bottle. "Here's luck to you, Will Turner!"

Elizabeth sat down next to the fire and took a bottle of rum herself. She forced down a sip and began to sing, "*Drink up, me hearties, yo ho . . .*"

"What – what was that?" Jack asked.

"It's nothing. A song I learned about pirates when I was a child," she told him.

"I know a lot of songs about pirates, but none

I'd teach a child," Jack said, tossing Elizabeth another bottle of rum. "Let's hear it."

Elizabeth began to sing, softly at first, but then more boldly:

"We pillage, we plunder, we rifle, we loot,
Drink up, me hearties, yo ho!

We kidnap, we ravage and don't give a hoot,
Drink up, me hearties, yo ho!

Yo ho, yo ho, a pirate's life for me,
Yo ho, yo ho, a pirate's life for me…"

"I *love* this song!" exclaimed Jack, and began to sing along.

"We're beggars and blighters and ne'er-do-well
cads,
Drink up, me hearties, yo ho!

Aye, but we're loved by our mums and
our dads,
Drink up, me hearties, yo ho!"

The two hoisted their bottles, but only Jack drank. Elizabeth pretended to.

"When I get the *Black Pearl* back, I'm going to teach it to the whole crew, and we'll sing it *all* the time," Jack promised, finishing off the bottle.

"You'll be positively the most fearsome pirates to sail the Spanish Main!" Elizabeth saluted.

"Not just the Spanish Main," Jack said dreamily, "the whole ocean . . . the whole world. Wherever we want to go, we go. That's what a ship is, you know. Not just a keel and a hull and a deck and sails. That's what a ship needs. But what a ship is . . . what the *Black Pearl* really is . . . is freedom!"

"To freedom!" said Elizabeth in a toast.

"To the *Black Pearl*!" said Jack, tapping his bottle against Elizabeth's. Jack happily took a last sip of rum, leaned back and fell asleep, dead drunk.

Jack awoke with a huge headache the next morning. He sat up slowly and rubbed his poor head. Suddenly, he was hit with a whiff of smoke.

He looked around. The whole island was on fire, and Elizabeth was busy pouring rum on the blaze.

"What are you doing?" yelled Jack, leaping to his feet. "You've burned our food, the shade . . . the rum! Why?"

Elizabeth calmly pointed to the smoke spiralling into the sky. "That signal goes up 1,000 feet . . . it can be seen for 200 leagues in every direction. The entire Royal Navy is out looking for me . . . . Do you think there's even a chance they could miss it?" she asked Jack, who was now furious.

"You . . . you burned up the island for a one-time chance of being saved?" he asked in disbelief.

"Exactly," she said.

Jack threw his hands up and stalked off in a huff. He climbed to the top of a dune and looked out to sea. He stared for a moment, shaking his head. Then, suddenly, on the horizon, he saw white sails. *Can't be!* he thought. But sure enough, it was. The *Dauntless* was heading towards the island. They'd seen the signal and were on their way to rescue Elizabeth.

"There'll be no living with her after this!" Jack grumbled to himself.

Chapter
20

Once again, Jack found himself on the deck of the *Dauntless*, and once again, Norrington was about to throw him in the brig.

But Elizabeth was still determined to save Will, and she knew she needed Jack to do it.

A number of sailors had gathered around Jack and were ready to clap him into irons when she said, "Commodore, we must set out immediately for Isla de la Muerta! Captain Sparrow can chart the course, but he won't from the brig."

Jack nodded in agreement. "Think about it," he said to Norrington. "The *Black Pearl* . . . Barbossa . . . the last real pirate threat in the Caribbean. How can you pass that up?"

Elizabeth could see that Commodore Norrington was not convinced, nor was her father. "We are returning to Port Royal, not gallivanting after pirates," Governor Swann told her.

"Then we're condemning Will to his death," she said, and turned to Norrington. "Commodore, I beg you. Please do this . . . for me . . . as a wedding gift."

Norrington was shocked. "Am I to understand that you will accept my proposal of marriage on the condition I rescue Mr Turner?" he asked.

"Not a condition," answered Elizabeth. "I will marry you."

Jack too was shocked!

"Mr Gillette," Commodore Norrington shouted to his first mate, "take Mr Sparrow to the bridge. He'll give you the heading."

Jack stood at the helm of the *Dauntless* and set it on course for Isla de la Muerta. He knew he had to hurry. He was in a race to get to the island before Will Turner's blood could finally turn Barbossa and his cursed crew into real men.

At the same moment, aboard the *Black Pearl*, Captain Barbossa appeared with Pintel and his one-eyed friend in front of Will's cell. "Bring him," he ordered.

Jack's crew was left in their cell as the pirates piled into a longboat. They rowed with Will at gunpoint through the fog and disappeared into the mouth of the cave.

Chapter
21

Commodore Norrington lowered his spyglass. The decks of the *Black Pearl* were empty. "I don't care for the situation," he said to Jack. "Any attempt to storm the island could turn into an ambush."

"Not if you do the ambushing," Jack answered. "I'll go in and convince Barbossa to send his men out . . . leaving you to do nothing but stand on the deck of the *Dauntless* and holler, 'Fire cannons'! What do you have to lose?" asked Jack, leaving out the minor detail of the curse that made Barbossa's crew immortal.

Norrington reluctantly agreed and allowed Jack to take a longboat to the island alone.

But watching Jack smile as he rowed away, he reconsidered. "Mr Gillette, break out the longboats."

Below decks, Governor Swann was knocking on Elizabeth's cabin door, but there was no answer. Elizabeth was standing before the open stern window. She had tied her bedsheets together and was lowering herself down to a rowing boat tied alongside the *Dauntless*. The governor knocked again. "Elizabeth!" he said, but she was gone. In the light of the full moon, she was rowing the small boat towards the *Black Pearl*.

Chapter
22

Inside the cave, lit by torches and shafts of moonlight, the pirates climbed over rocks and waded through water, pushing Will along.

"No reason to fret," Pintel told Will. "It's just the prick of a finger and a few drops of blood."

But another pirate was quick to correct him. "No mistakes this time," he said, looking at Will. "He's only half Turner. We spill it all!"

Pintel shrugged. "I guess there is a reason to fret." He giggled.

Will was shoved to his knees next to the Aztec stone chest at the centre of the cavern. A pirate pushed Will's head forward so that his neck was directly over the chest. Then Barbossa put a blade to his throat.

"Excuse me," came a voice. "Pardon me. Beg pardon."

Barbossa froze in anger. *Jack Sparrow!* He was making his way through the crowd of pirates. "Not possible," said Barbossa, gritting his teeth and staring at him.

"Not probable," said Jack, knowing anything was possible.

"Jack!" shouted Will, raising his head. But a pirate pushed it back down.

Barbossa pointed his knife at Jack. "You're next!" he said as he put the knife back to Will's throat.

"You don't want to be doing that," Jack said calmly.

Barbossa clenched his fists, not wanting to ask but knowing he had to. "*Why* don't I want to do this?"

"Because the HMS *Dauntless*, pride of the Royal Navy, is floating right offshore waiting for you," answered Jack. Barbossa took the knife from

Will's throat and turned toward Jack.

Jack pointed out that if the curse was lifted, Barbossa and his crew would become living men again . . . the kind Commodore Norrington and the Royal Navy would have no trouble killing. But if they rowed out to the *Dauntless* as the cursed men they were, they could have the *Dauntless* along with the *Pearl*!

"And there you are," said Jack, "with two ships! The makings of your very own fleet," he added. Jack now had Barbossa's full attention.

"Of course, you'll take the grandest as your flagship . . . and who's to argue?" smiled Jack as he strolled over to the chest and ran his fingers through the gold coins. "But what of the *Pearl*?" he pondered out loud. The question hung in the air as Barbossa stared at him.

"Make me captain," Jack suddenly offered. "I sail under your colours. I give you ten per cent of my plunder, and you get to introduce yourself at tea parties as Commodore Barbossa."

Barbossa set his jaw. "Fifty per cent," he answered.

"Fifteen," countered Jack.

"Forty," said Barbossa.

"Twenty-five," replied Jack. "And I'll buy you the hat."

Barbossa smiled. "We have an accord," he said, and the two shook hands.

Barbossa turned his attention from Will. He'd be saving the boy's blood for later, when Norrington and his men would be dead and safely out of the way. He glared triumphantly at his crew.

"Take a walk," he told them.

Chapter
23

Outside the cave, on the still, moonlit water, Commodore Norrington and an armed crew waited in seven longboats. They were planning a surprise attack on the pirates as they emerged from the cave.

The sailors never noticed the slight ripple that moved across the water. The pirates were moving out of the cave, all right, but they did not come out in longboats. They were walking across the sea bed!

Fish scattered in every direction as the shadowy figures, weapons in hands, trudged through the shifting current. Water-filtered moonlight made them an eerie army of marching skeletons. They silently walked under Norrington's longboats and headed for the *Dauntless* unseen.

The silence was broken by a sudden splash of water. Every sailor raised his pistol as a rowing boat slowly emerged from the mouth of the cave. Norrington looked at the two figures in the boat and ordered his men to hold their fire. He couldn't believe what he was seeing. Two women were rowing the boat!

On the deck of the *Dauntless*, Gillette was keeping watch with a spyglass. He saw the two women rowing from the cave. Then he saw one of them lower her parasol in the moonlight. They were two skeletons in women's dresses, and one of them had a wooden eye!

Realizing they'd been found out, one of the skeletons raised a pistol and shot the hat off the first mate's head. Gillette gasped as the skeleton pirates who had silently boarded the ship now dropped down from the rigging like spiders. The attack on the *Dauntless* had begun!

The sound of guns alerted Norrington to the fight on the *Dauntless*. He looked back and saw the ghostly skeletons running riot over the ship. He quickly ordered his men to row back to the *Dauntless*, but a sudden round of cannon fire blew one of the longboats to pieces. Norrington was now being fired upon by the cannons of his own ship!

The sailors rowed against the barrage of cannon with all their might, firing at the pirates on the *Dauntless* as they went. Finally, Norrington's boats pulled up alongside the ship. He and his men climbed up the side. They scrambled over the rails and joined the battle raging on deck.

Norrington suddenly found himself facing a huge pirate swinging an axe at his neck. He was battling the man back and over the side when Governor Swann grabbed him. "Elizabeth!" he exclaimed in a panic. "She's gone!"

Chapter
24

Elizabeth had reached the *Black Pearl*. Desperate to save Will, she silently began to climb up the side of the ship. Then she heard voices coming from the galley. Two pirates were busy preparing a grand feast of cakes, biscuits, rum and jerky. They were waiting for Barbossa and his crew to return to the *Black Pearl* with the good news that the curse was lifted and they would finally be able to taste real food as real men!

"Which would you eat first?" asked one pirate, eyeing the feast that was laid out on the table.

"Mmm, the cake!" answered the other.

"Aye, the cake!" they agreed as Elizabeth climbed past the porthole. The ship creaked as she climbed over the gunwale and sneaked along the deck. Suddenly, out of the darkness, the monkey dropped down in front of her and shrieked. Elizabeth grabbed him by the fur with her hands and tossed him over the side. Screeching as he fell, the monkey hit the water with a splash. The two pirates looked out the porthole and down into the water . . . then up to the deck.

Elizabeth ran, but she knew the pirates had seen her. She hid in a dark corner as they charged onto the deck. Suddenly, the two pirates heard the ropes in the sails move. Turning to see where the noise was coming from, they were struck in the chest by the boom of the ship. They flew overboard, where they joined the flailing monkey.

To Elizabeth's surprise, Jack's crew stepped out of the shadows. AnaMaria and Gibbs had swung the boom, sending the last two pirates into the sea below. The *Black Pearl* was theirs!

"All of you!" Elizabeth said, relieved to see them. "Will is in that cave, and as long as we have a chance to save him, we must act! And Jack, too!" she added, trying to lower a boat into the water.

But no one raised a hand to help her. Elizabeth looked at them, confused.

"Jack owes us a ship," said AnaMaria sternly.

"And we've got the *Pearl* . . ." added Gibbs. "And then there's the code to consider."

"The code?" asked Elizabeth in disbelief. "Falls behind, left behind . . ." she muttered. "You're pirates! Hang the code!"

But the crew was sticking by it, and Elizabeth rowed out to Isla de la Muerta alone.

Inside the cave, not knowing that his beloved ship was now sailing away, Jack examined the exquisite pirate treasure more carefully.

"You're a hard man to predict," Barbossa said, watching Jack hold up a gold-and-diamond necklace.

"Me?" Jack exclaimed as he shook his head. "I'm dishonest. A dishonest man can always be trusted to be dishonest," he explained. Then, as if to illustrate the point, Jack suddenly flipped a beautiful sword off the floor into Will's hands.

"Dang it, Jack!" howled Barbossa, who knew he was in for a fight. "I was almost liking you."

Jack grabbed a sword for himself and charged at Barbossa. The two squared off, sliding over the glittering gold coins that covered the cave's floor.

Another pirate slashed at Will, who managed to turn so the pirate's sword cut the ropes from his hands. With both hands free, Will took on three pirates at once.

The sound of clashing metal echoed through the cave as Jack and Barbossa fought furiously. Then Barbossa stepped back and began to laugh. He dropped his sword and grabbed Jack's blade with both hands. "You can't beat me, Jack." He laughed, then twisted the sword from Jack's grip and drove it into Jack's chest!

Will froze. Jack looked down at the sword jutting from his ribs and staggered back into the moonlight.

"Well, isn't that interesting," remarked Jack as his own body turned into a skeleton. "That curse seemed to be so useful," he said, taking a gold coin from his pocket, "I decided to get one for myself!"

Barbossa grabbed his sword as Jack pulled his own from his chest, and the two skeletons lunged and battled in the moonlight.

"So what now, Jack Sparrow?" asked Barbossa as they duelled over chests of gold, skull to skull. "Are we to be two immortals locked in battle until Judgment Day?"

"Or you could surrender," Jack suggested. But Barbossa wasn't interested, and fiercely continued his attack.

Will was trying to fight his way out of a corner when an explosion blinded him for a moment. Two pirates pounced and were about to make short work of him when one of them was suddenly gaffed in the back!

Will slashed at the other pirate and scrambled free to find Elizabeth holding the gaff. Back to back, they fought off the pirates together.

Frustrated beyond measure, Barbossa slashed at Jack and drove him backwards toward Elizabeth.

"I swear, Sparrow," he vowed, "when my men return, I will carve and joint your body and decorate the *Black Pearl* with the pieces!" Then he reached out and grabbed Elizabeth, putting his sword to her throat.

Jack stepped back, took out his pistol, and fired the one shot he'd been saving all those years.

Barbossa looked down at the hole in his shirt and back up at Jack.

"Ten years you carry that pistol and now you waste your shot?" the pirate captain asked him.

"He didn't waste it!" Will said triumphantly, standing over the chest of Aztec gold. He slashed his palm with his knife and wrapped his hand around the gold medallion. Then he dropped the bloody medallion into the chest.

Barbossa looked down at his chest as he began to bleed from the bullet hole. The pirate gave Jack a final snarl.

Jack tossed the pistol away and Barbossa fell to the floor, dead.

At that same moment, aboard the *Dauntless*, a pirate suddenly cried out and fell to the deck. Two more stepped into the moonlight and realized they were no longer skeletons. The curse was lifted, but it was too soon for Barbossa's men.

All around the ship, pirates fell quickly to Norrington's men, and those who did not surrendered.

"Parley?" asked Pintel hopefully as he and Ragetti were led to the brig.

In the meantime, Jack had some unfinished business inside the cave of Isla de la Muerta. Using his knife, he cut his arm, then wiped the blood from the blade onto the gold coin. He held the coin over the chest but couldn't quite bring himself to drop it.

"The immortal Captain Jack Sparrow," he said dreamily. "It has a ring."

"Oh, well," he sighed, thinking better of the idea, and he dropped the coin into the chest. He then gathered some large gold pieces from the cave and happily climbed into a longboat with Will and Elizabeth. "If I could trouble you to drop me at the *Black Pearl* . . ."

But when they reached the mouth of the cave, Jack stood up in the longboat and saw that the *Black Pearl* was gone. He scanned the water, but it was no good.

"I'm sorry," Will told him as Jack sat back down.

Jack knew what his crew had done, but he bore them no grudge. "They did what's right by them," he said, knowing he would soon be on his way to meet the hangman in Fort Charles.

Chapter
25

Jack's luck finally seemed to have failed him as he stood on the wooden gallows, the hangman's noose around his neck.

Elizabeth and her father, along with Commodore Norrington, were in the crowd for the proceedings. "This is wrong," Elizabeth pleaded. "He risked his life to rescue me, and then risked it again to save your crew." But in her father's eyes, the law was the law, and in the Crown's eyes, Jack had broken it.

Will was also on hand, moving through the crowd that had come to see the pirate hang. As the drums began to roll and the executioner moved his hand towards the lever, Will noticed a green bird landing on a ledge. It was Cotton's parrot! It looked directly at Will –

it was a signal – and Will gave Jack a nod.

Will stepped up to Elizabeth and drew his sword. "I love you," he told her. "I should have told you a long time ago."

Before she could say a word, Will dashed to the gallows, drawing a second sword as the executioner pulled the lever. Will leaped to the stairs of the gallows and buried his sword in the top of the trap door. It opened and Jack fell. But the sword stuck sideways from the trap door, and Jack's feet found it before he was hanged.

Jack balanced on the blade. Will swung his sword and severed the hangman's rope, freeing Jack, who pulled the sword from the trap door as he fell; then he hit the ground, brandishing the weapon.

Jack and Will battled Norrington's guards under the gallows until they reached the parapet of the fort. But with the sea at their backs, they had nowhere left to go. The troops raised their rifles. Jack and Will were cornered.

Suddenly, Will stepped up and put himself between Jack and the armed guards. They'd have to shoot him before they could get to Jack.

Governor Swann pushed to the front with Norrington. "I granted you clemency and this is how you repay me?" he demanded of Will. "You throw in with *him*? He is a pirate!"

"And a good man!" Will shouted to Norrington.

"You forget your place, Turner," said the commodore.

"It's right here, between you and Jack," Will replied.

Elizabeth pushed her way through the crowd and jumped onto the parapet next to Will. "As is mine!" she declared.

"This is where your heart truly lies, then?" Norrington asked Elizabeth.

"It is," Elizabeth said.

Jack, Will and Elizabeth stared at Norrington. For a moment his eyes glinted with fierce determination. Then they could all see his face soften as he looked at Elizabeth. It was obvious that he realized the folly of their showdown. She would never love him the way she loved Will.

"I was rooting for you, mate," Jack said, giving Norrington a nod of condolence. Then he turned to the crowd and shouted, "Friends, this is the day you will always remember as the day you *almost* hung . . ." But before he could finish, Jack slipped off the parapet and tumbled into the sea below.

The crowd hurried to the stone wall. Jack could be seen swimming through the water. Sailing into the harbour, the crowd also saw the *Black Pearl*. Standing on her deck was Jack's crew, come back to save their captain!

Turning to Will, Norrington said, "This is a very nice sword. I expect the man who made it to show the same care and devotion to all aspects of his life." He saluted Will with the sword and added, "My compliments."

He then turned to Elizabeth and said cheerfully, "Miss Swann. The best of luck to you both."

Gillette raced up to the commodore and asked if he should prepare the *Dauntless* to pursue Jack.

"I think we can afford him one day's head start," Norrington replied with a smile. "More sporting that way."

On the parapet, Will and Elizabeth gazed into each other's eyes for a long moment. Then Will swept her up into his arms and kissed her.

"But he's a blacksmith," grieved the poor governor.

"No," said Elizabeth proudly. "He's a pirate!"

Chapter
26

From the fantail of the *Black Pearl*, Cotton, with his parrot on his shoulder, threw a line to Jack.

Jack grabbed the line as it swept by, and climbed to the deck of the *Black Pearl*. Gibbs greeted him with a salute.

"I thought I told you to keep to the code," Jack said to him seriously.

Gibbs shuffled his feet. "They're more what you might call guidelines . . ." he offered. Jack smiled. He continued up to the bow, where AnaMaria was standing at the wheel. She stepped away and said, "Captain Sparrow . . . the *Black Pearl* is yours."

Jack lovingly ran his hand along the rail, then took the wheel of the ship – his ship. He opened his compass and set his course. Satisfied with himself, he looked out to sea and began to sing himself a tune.

"*Yo ho, yo ho, a pirate's life for me . . .*"

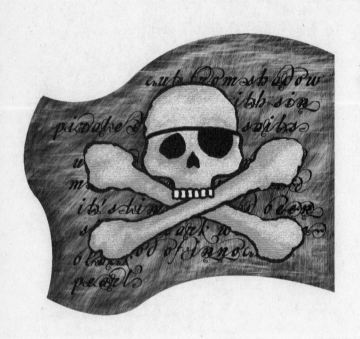